To..

with a heart full of love

Love is all around Oklahoma

Copyright © 2016 by Sourcebooks, Inc.
Written by Wendi Silvano
Illustrated by Joanna Czernichowska
Design by Quadrum Solutions (www.quadrumltd.com)

Sourcebooks and the colophon are registered trademarks of Sourcebooks, Inc.
All rights reserved. No part of this book may be reproduced in any form or by any electronic or mechanical means including information storage and retrieval systems—except in the case of brief quotations embodied in critical articles or reviews—without permission in writing from its publisher, Sourcebooks, Inc.

Published by Sourcebooks Jabberwocky, an imprint of Sourcebooks, Inc.
P.O. Box 4410, Naperville, Illinois 60567-4410
(630) 961-3900
Fax: (630) 961-2168
www.sourcebooks.com

Source of Production: Phoenix Color, Hagerstown, Maryland
Date of Production: August 2015
Run Number: 5004410
Printed and bound in the United States of America.
PHC 10 9 8 7 6 5 4 3 2 1

Love is all around Oklahoma

Written by Wendi Silvano
Illustrated by Joanna Czernichowska

sourcebooks
jabberwocky

Love is a feeling that comes from inside.

Everyone feels it. It can't be denied.

But how do we know that it's there? What's the clue?

How can we see it?

Just what can we do?

Love's all around, if you just pay attention, in people and places too many to mention. Go look at the park, on the street, at the mall. You'll see love all over. It's big and it's small!

Around Oklahoma, in cars and on trains,

in taxis and buses, on boats and on planes,

in Tulsa, and Norman,

and Bartlesville too,

you'll find there is love that will come into view.

Right there, on the lawn, in cool Hafer Park

is a mom with her babe,

hearing songs of a lark.

At a store in Stillwater, a girl gets a bear.
She squeezes him,
squishes him,
ruffles his hair.

It's clear that she **loves** him. She's **smiling** and bright.
She tucks him in **softly** and **gently** at night.

That same little girl, the very next day,
sees a **friend** at her school who is too **sad** to play.

So she sits down beside him and listens and shares, making sure that he knows there's someone who cares.

Now the boy who was **sad** feels much **better**, you see,
so he runs home all happy to play with **Magee**.
They **romp** and they **frolic**.
They **fetch** and they **run**.
It's certain he **loves** him. They're having such **fun**!

You can see how **love** travels when **shared** with a friend.
If ***everyone*** shares love, it never will end.
From one to another, it s p r e a d s and it **grows**.
You can't have ***too much***, as everyone knows.

An officer in Edmond who **helps** change a flat.

A fireman in Lawton who **rescues** a cat.

CHESAPEAKE ENERGY ARENA

The home team that makes the crowd **cheer** and **clap**.
Each moment has **love** like a **gift** you unwrap.

There's a **father** who sits at the table each night, **helping** out with the homework to get it just **right**.

He's tired and busy, but that's **love**, you know...

giving up what you want to **help** someone else **grow**.

It's not only *people* who show love, it's true.

Just come see the creatures that play at the zoo!

The polar bear tumbles and rolls with her cub,

and when they are finished, she gives him a rub.

Where else is there love? Have we looked all around?

I think we've forgotten—love grows from the ground!

In the meadows and gardens and parks you will find

that the earth shows us love of all shapes and all kinds.

Wherever you look, **love** comes into sight.

It's there in the morning, it's there in the night.

But in all **Oklahoma**,

the best love you'll find

is a **love** that is **gentle**,

and **selfless**, and **kind**…

It's the love found at home. It shows up each day in things people do and in things people say. There's no greater love, I can tell you, it's true, than the love of your family...

Especially for YOU!